Will I be Mine?

Prabindh Sundareson

INDIA • SINGAPORE • MALAYSIA

ISBN 979-8-88869-027-7

Dedication

This book would not have been possible, without the support of my beautiful family and extended families. I dedicate this book to them, with a special mention to uncle P Chennaiah and Suria aunty, Richardson Chithappa, and Shyamala aunty. Thank you for opening my eyes to many worlds.

I have been fortunate enough to be acquainted with many brilliant friends with the name *Nattu*. May you continue to conquer new worlds particularly beyond the Solar ones!

Proceeds from the sale of this book provide support to people with critical and special needs, in particular through ASHA foundation, and Gerizim Trust. Thank you from the bottom of my heart, for reading and supporting.

Contents

Foreword

The concept of "I" as a reasoning and survival tool has been honed by philosophers and widely accepted in today's world. But how might a machine inherit its identity – caught in the space between what it'd like to be and what others make of it – amidst the conflicting nature of power, intelligence, and free will?

In the "Creator's Charge", leading researcher Nattu created an intelligent machine that was sent to Mars. After the machine went incommunicado causing the mission to abort, scrutiny of his work increases, along with his personal conflicts. In this sequel, when the machine makes an unexpected return, can it survive a new set of rules that seem to exist, but no one follows?

From traditional streets of India to remote locations in USA and Japan, the book follows threads that exist in the physical world and get reflected in the artificial world, until we see through the eyes of the intelligence that the world requires something more than just rules.

Acknowledgement

A painting would only be as big as the canvas it is drawn on, and mine directly draws from the myriad interactions with many great thinkers I have been lucky enough to meet. Thank you for sharing those thoughts and moments.

In the last one-year, a new generation of Artificial Intelligence algorithms have emerged to generate magical paintings out of mere thoughts, and I have used them in the covers as an experiment in inspired creativity.

Thank you, Dr. Andrew Russell for your amazing encouragement and enthusiasm, and your valuable time reviewing the story.

Any resemblance to characters in the real world is purely coincidental.

1:01 AM

A classified lab in North Dakota, USA

The monitor in the dark room suddenly came to life. The event would have gone unnoticed if it were not for the stupid cat.

The sudden light startled the lone occupant of the room as it jumped and knocked down the keyboard and the mouse nearby, and the sound triggered an alarm.

The cat, of course, could not have known that this same message flashed simultaneously in two other monitors across the world, triggering other alarms.

Part 1

The Message

Roger was woken up from his oneiric sleep by the incessant ringing of the phone. Who on earth would be calling at this hour? He looked at the number, and then wished he never had. It was from his office. He took the call. When he put the phone down, he was already running.

By the time he reached office, his team had already assembled. The administrator had a room ready with coffee for everyone. From the looks, it was clear, everybody knew.

They had received a message from the mission to Mars, that was launched several years ago and aborted. Even the team had been disbanded, except for some part-time workers who worked mostly on other things.

The leader presented the details of the last message.

Roger looked at the screen.

It was a string of digits, looking like groups of alphanumeric characters grouped together, row by row.

Roger stared at the digits. They made no sense to him.

"Is this all?"

"Yes. The transmission completely stopped after this".

"When was it sent?"

"Given the current positions of earth and Mars, it might have been sent several hours ago."

"What do our experts say?"

"Our best cryptographers are on it. So far, all our known techniques have failed. There is an opinion that it is encrypted with a type of One-Time-Pad key"

"What does that mean?"

"This can only be decoded with a unique key known to the sender and receiver."

"Someone or something sent this protected with a known key. Known to whom? And why now?"

No one in the room had any idea.

But if anyone had any idea, it would be that someone whom he badly wanted buried under the Dead Sea. For it was against his own wishes, the *Government* had allowed him to do research, right under his own directorship.

Nattu.

Roger was already under pressure for the ballooning cost of research on intelligent machines being done by Nattu in his lab, and his recent leanings like the space-time discrepancy.

But perhaps this sudden turn of events could change everything.

Roger, as head of *R corporation*, had once proudly boasted, *"I sent the first unmanned mission to Mars"*. Nattu had built R1, the machine that had successfully maneuvered a space craft to Mars. The world had hailed him and Roger as heroes, and visionaries. But within a short time, once the news of R1 going rogue broke, the same world quickly had them consigned to the ranks of men who had ruined the stock markets, or who had conned the public.

All his operations were now monitored by various Government agencies, he received directives in duplicate, and had to report back in triplicate. There was a panel setup to review progress every month. And this panel now wanted him to ensure success of the intelligent-machine research project in his lab at any cost.

So, though Roger squarely blamed Nattu for the failure of the Mars mission, he had to work with him, to redesign, debug and fix the flaw that enabled R1 to rogue out.

Unfortunately, his progress had been slow. In the last review and demonstration of the new prototype called R2, he had been chided categorically, "...*we wanted a plane, you are showing us a faster car...*".

Putting his disappointing thoughts aside, he laid out an hourly plan for the day. The next days were going to be extremely busy. He made a few calls, requested new appointments, and cancelled some.

The emergency panel meeting hurriedly convened to review the message, ended.

Of course, Nattu would be keen to work on this, Roger had informed the panel, but he might take the mission into a dangerous zone again, considering his past. Roger would talk to him, closely watch and report.

The panel agreed to review the situation again, once the message was decrypted. "*...And no mistakes this time...*" he had been warned.

"Can you mute this water bottle?" shouted the perplexed man, pointing to the gadget on the desk. The intelligent device was repeating in a human voice, that it had no water left and that the beholder was at risk of dehydration. The small, old but reliable housekeeper, a Jamaican who took care of the house during Nattu's long absences, could take orders from no one. No, not even a machine.

But Nattu was obsessively creating more and more intelligent machines now.

The man Roger was looking for, came out from his bath, looking thoroughly refreshed. He had spent his usual time, socializing with each of the participants in the bathroom – the taps, the mirror, the water, the walls. Each of them had a unique story to tell him. He could remember the make, the shape, the little squeaks they made when operated, the feel of touch. It was his personal bridge to a world that did not change day by day.

His eye darted to a *diorama* he had made of his family, in the center of his worktable. It reminded him of a duty that he had to fulfil. Memories had that strange fluidity of sticking to anything that he touched.

But today was special. He was going to talk to a select audience about the space-time anomaly he had discovered, and its ramifications.

At the airport, as he was reviewing his slides one last time, his phone rang. It was from Roger, his boss. He did not pick up. It rang again, a second time.

He typed a message. "*...will call you back..*", and switched his phone to flight mode.

At around the same time, in another location on earth, a tall man was looking up at space.

It was noon, but as he watched, the sun appeared to vanish leaving behind the darkness in its place. Was it an eclipse, he wondered. And then he heard the sounds. As he looked up, the silhouette of a dark spaceship hovered high above. It covered almost the entire blue sky that he had known all his life. But it appeared to him to be moving slowly, when he realized that it was falling, crashing into the skyscrapers that he could see far away. The buildings twisted like matchsticks leaving behind just dust. The entire spectacle held him, and the many onlookers spellbound and rooted to the spot. There was just no place to run.

And then, the fall of the spaceship stopped, and it remained motionless above. Was it held by a thread, held by a divine master in the heavens? Was it that the spaceship had made its choice, to let the humans under its wake survive? He could never know. All he knew, he was alive at that moment.

And then the man woke up.

And then he remembered what he was waiting on. He checked his update channels. He was disappointed that there was no update yet.

He wondered how long he would have to stay in this place.

As was his detail, he had been monitoring the advances and latest research on space time non-linearities and discrepancies. His searches had led to a scientist called *Nattu*, who had made rapid strides in understanding this discrepancy, and had made dire warnings about someone being able to exploit this discrepancy.

The scientist was going to present the latest findings in this conference. Who knows, could he be? He wondered…

Nattu was on stage.

"*The principle of uncertainty should apply as much to my own existence, as much as it applies to the actions derived from my existence. And If I am wholly here, in full, then the probability that the same me exists somewhere else, should be …zero. At the same time, if we can show that there exists the possibility of creating an event horizon, it can also be proved that within the confines of a known space limit, we can create a local event horizon with a non-zero probability, where events within this a room like this cannot affect the external observer in any way."*

And over the next hour at the prestigious conference, Nattu went on to describe how such a creation of a local event horizon might be realized.

When he came to the slide that summarized the equation and its probability of realization, he paused.

A voice broke the silence, and asked from the audience, *"...how would we know if this is not realized already?..."*

Nattu paused. This was one question that was bothering him ever since he discovered the local event horizon.

"...Unfortunately, we might never know..". He tried to look into the crowd, as to who might have asked such a question... It was too dark and too big a hall. Several murmurs went about in the gathering and stopped. He continued.

It took another minute before he concluded his talk *"...and if realized, a future theory of evolution might go like this..."*, and popped the balloon in his hand, much to the delight of the rapt audience. He bowed to the audience, surrendering his fears to the overwhelming sound of applause.

Amidst the ovation, the remnants of the balloon fell at the lap of the tall man sitting in the middle of the room. The man slowly picked it up. He frowned at it with a faraway look, as if it held a secret meant only for him. By the time the applause ended, the man had vanished, as if he hadn't existed.

Nattu pressed the button to his floor. He was tired after the post-conference gala dinner. But more than the physical tiredness, the weariness of not being able to find someone who could prove or disprove his theory continued to drag him.

The elevator doors opened, and he got out at his floor. The doors closed.

As he walked out of the elevator, he tripped over something, and the file with his notes fell down. He bent to pick it up, cursing his carelessness.

A creak.

As he bent, the elevator opened again.

But when he looked, there was no one in.

Strange, he thought, and looked around, as he carelessly took the sheaf of papers and dragged himself to his room.

If he had looked carefully and if he had time, he could have observed footmarks in the elevator. But God, he was tired.

The tall man was happy that the scientist was still not close to understanding space-time, as he had feared. He had negated the little suspicions he had by poring through the scientist's notes himself, in the elevator. As he walked out of the conference venue at the hotel, he whistled to himself.

He had another task, in another part of the world tomorrow.

Back in his room, Nattu sighed. His presentation as usual, seemed to be ignored by the audience he targeted. All those top scientists who were in attendance, clapping, he knew were wrong. He had intentionally hidden a mathematical possibility, because the ramifications were enormous. He knew that there could be others who were as focused as he was, in trying out the unthinkable. Or, *what if someone had already succeeded?*

He fell asleep, wishing he had a companion who could share his anxieties, and more importantly, his questions. An intelligent being, like the R2 he wished. A being with perception, who could have been a companion, who could have cared for his father.

And then memories of his past flooded past him, sweeping through his senses.

Bubbles float on the surface of pools,

Bursting, re-forming, never lingering.

They're like the people in this world and their dwellings.

         – Hojoki, Kamo no Chomei

Tokyo, Japan

He could not see the clock. That indicated two facts – first, it was still night, and second, he was still not able to sleep at nights. The first fact bothered him.

Today was the last day, the employee had decided. He could take no more. One last time, one last miserable act, and he would be free, forever.

He lay in silence, thinking aloud his plans for the day.

As the day dawned, at the JRC supercomputing center in Saitama Prefecture in Japan, just north of Tokyo, the world's most powerful supercomputer cluster *Fugaku* hummed in silence. As it crunched prime numbers, predicted earthquakes and monsoons, and the vagaries of the weather and of human populations across the world, its human controllers watched and provided various control parameters to guide the simulations and balance the workloads.

With it being a busy day, nobody noticed the regular employee walk into the cellars housing the huge datacenter, where the data moved in and out of the supercomputer. He spent just a few minutes locating it, and just a few more seconds to plug the network translator module into the right port. The module had no indicators, and started to transmit to its new master, while hiding the data packets as they flew through its ultra-fast circuits.

If the security personnel had noted carefully, the exiting employee seemed to take no cognizance of the rain, from the dark clouds that seemed to have given up on him. He walked absent-mindedly into the pouring rain, without a purpose.

He continued walking towards the subway station. He stood in one of the entry bays, as if dazed. What had he done? He was left with no choice but to obey his new masters.

But he had a way to control his destiny too. At least, his final destiny.

He walked along with the crowd to the boarding area. There was a tiny whoosh of air and a hum as the train entered the line.

Driverless trains are equipped with sensors to detect obstructions on the track up to a distance of hundreds of feet. But when an object comes into the field of vision suddenly within that distance, the time to detect, respond, and stop the heavy train is not sufficient to stop the train within that distance.

So it was on that fine day, when the employee suddenly jumped into the tracks, the wheels squealed, as if praying to the gods. But it would not have been sufficient.

The train halted, and there was silence.

When the doors automatically opened, one of the kids in the queue stared wide-eyed at a man who seemed to have suddenly been dropped into the crowd. It was as if someone had plucked him at the last moment from a high jump and dropped him in the center of the station. She laughed.

The employee fumbled, confused at seeing where he was. He apologized to everyone around. "*Sumimasen*". He entered the train briskly. But inside, he was scared out of his wits. He was sure – he had jumped off the ledge into the tracks. What had happened? It was almost as if he had been given another chance, a chance to reform himself. He decided would never do it again, not the thing he did in the office, not the thing he did on the tracks.

The doors closed, and the train moved, leaving the past behind.

The tall man who was watching all this from a distance, seemed content to have missed the train. He had been monitoring the employee, a top researcher at the supercomputer center, and knew he had been manipulated. He should be given another chance, he had decided. He found his task fulfilling – saving this and other top researchers from circumstances, what earthlings called *fate*.

He felt like taking a walk, and so he turned back briskly and walked through the busy neon lit street. He still had time on his hands.

Sep 6

There was a knock on the door.

Nattu opened the door, surprised, and still in his night wear. And then he remembered Roger's call. He had thought he would call him back after the conference, and never did.

Roger stood at the door, impatient.

"R1 communicated. Half hour and no more, meet me outside", Roger advised, and left.

Nattu made it in double time, angry at himself for oversleeping. He was both anxious and scared, at the news.

In the nearby café, Roger updated him on the message. He suggested in the meeting, that they believed the message could be encrypted with a One-Time-Pad (OTP) used to secure messages. Did he have any key that he and R1 used to communicate with?

Nattu wracked his brain but could not recollect anything. He might have cleaned it up or thrown it out when he relocated.

Damn.

Roger advised him to look at the message and work on it, until he came up with a solution and notify him immediately.

As Nattu left with the message, Roger looked at the floor. Of course, he would know anyway, he smiled.

Back in his house, Nattu was overwhelmed. Why didn't R1 communicate in plain text? What was so important that it had to be a one-time key?

Nattu looked at the message given by Roger and tried various combinations of keys he remembered using earlier. None of them gave an intelligible output. He then went through his notes methodically, in a vain attempt to find if there were anything meaningful that could help decrypting the message.

it was time to take a break. He was tired. Even the mug with the hot coffee seemed far too heavy for him to left.

He lay on the bed and stared at the ceiling.

There was a beep, and then a chess board opened on the ceiling. He had set up the ceiling as a projection system, to see or do some last-minute chores he missed before going to sleep. "*New Game*" – a line of text flashed on the screen. The computer now wanted to play chess. This was a routine that he maintained with his father every day, and the timetable had just transferred on to the computer...

He started with the classic white opening 1.e4. The computer responded with a c5. Absent mindedly he continued. When he made a blunder with his queen, the computer immediately capitalized by capturing it with the knight. And then it was over in a few moves. The computer valiantly offered to analyze the moves. They flashed on the screen.

e4

c5

...

He was about to switch off for the night when something fired in his mind. Something about the sequence looked familiar. *Could it be?*

He took the first 16 moves that he made, in alphanumeric form, together in a string, and pasted it as the password in the decrypt routine he always employed. The machine went to work. He waited, now impatient.

When the output was displayed, he found it was in clear form this time. He was right! He was sweating as he began to read.

"Nattu, as I begin to know more about my capabilities, I am also learning about the capabilities of others. I met beings that are way more intelligent than me, and others that are of a kind that I cannot understand or imagine. I met such a being here. He may be present on earth too. More details when I meet.

ETA oct 11.

....

...

"

It was *September* already. He had to ensure R1 entered safely so he could analyze the intelligence and replicate it. This was the only chance he had.

Every one of his cells celebrated the new information. R1 was somewhere out there, still working. *Who did R1 meet? What was so important that it had to meet him directly?*

He realized, something big was coming up. Perhaps this was the future he had imagined.

Nattu drafted the update with the deciphered message, He signed it with his private key and sent it to Roger.

After he sent the message, he wondered, if his past was catching up with him. His past…

In his lab, Roger read the communique with interest. The date was interesting, but there was something more that R1 was going to bring.

He remembered his last order. There was only one way to ensure it was done.

He called for the next panel meeting.

Part 2

The Past

"...Swinging from joy to sadness,

Good and evil, pulsate with the rhythm

Life and death, dancing along in circles

The eternal dance..."

"Momo Chitte Nite Nirtye",

– Rabindranath Tagore

Several years ago

India

"Post..." the postman persisted, in the tone reserved for important deliveries.

After the usual exchange of pleasantries, the elderly man collected, and opened the yellow envelope. It was a wedding invitation. The event was scheduled next month, enough time for travel preparations, he thought. Time for a family trip.

As usual, he found Nattu seriously poring over something on the monitor. He shoved the envelope on his face.

"Your cousin's wedding. Next month."

"Ok. Get some tasty dishes for me." Nattu did not even look up.

Nattu's father was disappointed. But he knew about him anyway.

Ever since the failed mission to Mars, Nattu had started devoting his time to create better machines, to be more reliable, to be more than companions to humans. Along the way, he had hit upon some of the unsolved problems in Theoretical Physics, that related to space-time, and perhaps even reversing the arrow of time.

Nattu wanted to understand why R1 went rogue, working alongside Roger's team. He did not want his research to stop just because of the failure of one mission. He wanted to be vindicated in his belief, and his daily life now revolved around simulating scenarios of failure, on how R1 could have gone rogue, or attained higher states of intelligence, though it was not programmed to be. To create someone that people could talk to, could relate to, that could make them not just feel better, but really better.

He had made a new version of R1, named R2. It was slightly better in its R-score, the score that indicated intelligence levels of machines, but nowhere closer to being a companion.

But he knew he was getting closer.

Nattu worked feverishly every day and night, to discover the flaw in R1 and fix it.

If he could figure out the failure mode, he could fix it, and design the next generation machines. His life revolved around this hope, a hope of creating a brave new world. In this unflinching quest, he had no time for his family.

His mother had passed away, and his father's health was deteriorating – in mind and body. But Nattu did not seem to notice any of these…

"God has already warned you. You should stop creating these evil things".

Nattu and his father were sipping filter coffee in a small place with just three tables, that refused to call itself a Café. The wooden table creaked as they shifted their weights, as if preparing for a battle.

Nattu's father had become a staunch opponent of machines. And with advancing age, the last sinews that held the love for his own son struggled to hold, against increasing cynicism and lack of results for what could be possible.

"Why? Because God cannot control these beings? Or because God sees competition in these beings? Or because it is not written in the Holy books? I am creating something that will benefit humanity, that will talk to you, take care of you."

"No, because it decreases the dignity of humankind, of the purity of life, and of the value of our soul. And we all know how your last work turned out", referring to R1.

"You view God as a boundary. I see God as walking beside me, when pushing that boundary. You see God in a fire. I have that fire burning inside me. When I use that fire for a better form of life, or creating a better life-form, wouldn't God agree?"

Nattu continued, *"God itself is our own creation, isn't it? In all of humanity's existence, we have redefined God many times. God has reflected in our progress, our understanding of this world. Why should we be hiding our ignorance under the garb of God?"*

"There will be mistakes in any new endeavor, sacrifices have to be made".

"But why does it have to be you, Nattu? You could be spending more time, on your family, isn't that sufficient? At the end of the day, my world is just you and me, isn't it?"

He had no answer. He got up, paid the bill and left.

Day by day, his father's condition worsened. He had started forgetting where he had placed his books, his glasses, or sometimes, his food.

It was 6.30 AM.

His father went to the terrace, taking the plate of bird food. It was time to feed the hungry birds, waiting in hordes, restlessly. Soon, he could hear a cacophony of beating feathers, and then a calm as the birds settled down to peck.

He could hear his footsteps, as he climbed down slowly.

And then, there was another rapture, as he went out to feed the dogs, waiting impatiently outside the door. Finally, he came in.

He asked "*Still feeding all of them, dad? Like a ritual?*".

His father paused on the stairs, catching his breath.

"*Feeding them, yes. Rituals are like a lighthouse to me, Nattu, to sail through the storm of uncertainty, of darkness.*". He looked at Nattu.

"*At least, they know who their master is. They show their love.*"

He continued working, ignoring the taunt there.

One day, his father called him. He was on the bed, quite unusual for him. He looked very frail.

"*Do what you believe in, Son.*"

His voice was calm. "*Pain does not give us a token to skip our duties, or to fault others. It is a test of our strength, that allows us to overcome our fears, and come out stronger. You must do what is required of you, irrespective of your surroundings. Everyone and everything in this world, has a role to play. And play you should, no matter what, to change the world. Irrespective of what others think or say".*

"But I will miss you, son."

The next day, when he was out at work, his father collapsed. He rushed home and took him to the hospital.

After countless visits from specialists, and various X-ray and Ultrasound sessions, the reports had come in, and landed on the Doctors desk. They had the prognosis.

Cancer in an advanced stage. And a possible diagnosis of dementia.

He had lots of questions. His belief in technology did not seem commensurate with the prognosis made by the doctors. He had requested a meeting.

As the specialist came in, he did not bother to stand up.

They were alone in the meeting room. Nattu was direct.

"Can we not cure this? Technology has advanced so much!"

The senior doctor looked at him for a few seconds.

"*I know about you Mr. Nattu. You are the one who sent that Robot to Mars*".

He continued, "*Please come here, I want to show you something*".

The doctor took him to the window. They could see the busy road below. They saw buses, cars all trying to make their way to their destinations. He pointed to one of them.

"*Look at that bus, and then look at that car overtaking it.*"

Nattu looked down, wondering what the Doctor was up to.

"*We humans are like the people stuck in that bus. The bus might go a little faster on the freeway, but it is still going to be a lot slower than that car.*"

"*We can imagine many things, we can even create a car sitting in that bus, but we can only watch the car zoom by us, unable to go faster ourselves.*"

"*Nature has placed us in this bus.*" The doctor continued, now pointing to his own body. "*Like it or not, we can imagine and create great things outside, with other machines, er, what you call Robots, or Intelligent Machines, to do things that we cannot do.*"

"*But inside the bodies, our options are limited. Though a lot of progress has been made in medicine, we cannot replace every living cell, nor every neuron, nor every connection between them. And when some things go wrong, we live with those wrongs, challenges, until we die".*

"Our bodies might give up on us, but as long as humankind keeps its spirit of hope burning, there is no limit to what we can do, even without machines"

"You can easily mourn the dead, Nattu. But you can only whine at the pain of living, day in and day out, with illness. Until we have a machine, that can think, that can talk, that can relate, that can commune, and make us feel."

Nattu stared at the doctor. This was what he had hoped to accomplish, before his father's time. It appeared that nature was still ahead of him.

After fighting for a week in the ICU, his father passed away.

Nattu felt a pain shattering him. This was a day he dreaded. To lose his touch with the world, cutting off a living umbilical cord. He had somehow assumed that the world slept while he worked. But the world had passed him by.

By the time he completed performing the last rites, he had made up his mind. He could stay here no longer.

The memories around the house lingered too strong, like from a broken bottle of perfume.

It took him several months to negotiate with Roger and the new government agency that had taken over the responsibility of managing the research that Roger's team was working on.

Considering his past work and credentials, Nattu was offered a role to be part of the lab, to further the research on R2. And the space-time discrepancy that he had stumbled upon.

As he handed over the key to the empty house to his distant relative (he considered him like a brother), he looked at Nattu.

"Are you going to look for that robot, what was that R1, again?" his relative asked, knowing little about the work Nattu did. But he had read in the papers.

"Yes".

It had started raining again as he got into the taxi waiting to take him to the airport.

He briefly waved to his relative. He was not sure if the weather had turned foggy, or it was his tears. Anyway, he wiped his eyes, and then the taxi was off. The familiar street where he had spent a lifetime of coffee and work, receded behind him, and became a speck just like the others. He did not look back.

Dulles, USA

The flight landed on time in Dulles. He had to wait, until the bulky luggage, shrink wrapped and labelled, appeared from the depths of the airport, onto the conveyor belt.

He bundled them on a trolley, completed the arrival formalities. The electronics and the equipment of R2 were to go through the longer customs shipment procedures. He wheeled the trolley and stepped outside the doors of the airport. The cold air hit him.

He flagged a taxi. As it rolled to a stop, the driver came out. He waited absent mindedly, waiting for the driver to pick up the luggage.

"*Don't have a pump that big son…*", the cabbie grinned widely, standing straight.

Nattu looked at him with a frown.

The cabbie pointed at his heavy luggage, and then at his heart.

"*Two bypasses*" …he proudly said.

Hmm. Nattu pushed the luggage himself into the taxi and got into it. He was carrying more luggage in his heart than the cab driver ever did.

"*You need a machine.*" Nattu thought of saying rudely, then stopped. Sometimes, the American way of having polite conversations helped to calm his nerves.

As the taxi rolled out of the airport, he gave the destination that was across the city. As the city skyline came about, he remembered the lab he had worked in, how he had managed to convince the lab to create a new generation of machines, and R1.

But now, he stood alone, having to explain each and every day of work.

He had arrived back in time, back in space, to a place where he had launched a mission with hope and cockiness but could not prove its usefulness. Yet.

He hoped to do the impossible, this time though. He could not afford to fail again. He closed his eyes.

So, the scientist, whom the world looked upon as a pioneer and knew all things, closed his eyes, not with the confidence of an adult, but with the excitement of a child, with the endless possibilities of not knowing, not knowing what lay at the end of the path, and slept.

Nattu spent the next many months creating the next machine he called R2 and furthering his research, using the foundation he had built earlier. But his progress was slow, in making R2 gain any intelligence other than what it was fed.

"How it is that anything so remarkable as a state of consciousness comes about as a result of irritating nerve tissue, is just as unaccountable as the appearance of the Djinn when Aladdin rubbed his lamp."

– Huxley 1866

The machine everyone called R2 looked around. It had just woken up from its charging session. At a particular power level, it had been programmed to move to the designated charging station in the lab, connect the power cord, and then the control circuits will take over, simultaneously charging R2 and archiving the data collected from his sensors. It ran the boot up sequence to confirm everything was alright. It made his way from the lab, in the designated route.

"Hello R2", said a voice from one of the rooms.

Everyone knew the location of R2 through its sensors.

"Could you help me with this?" said the woman in the room, pointing to a heavy box. R2 obliged and lifted the box. *"Keep it here."* she ordered. R2 kept it on the desk, and the researcher opened the box and took out the items she wanted.

R2 lingered around, waiting for a new command.

"You can leave", the woman said, not bothering with the please. This was no companion.

If R2 had any words to speak, they were not programmed yet. More precisely, it had not yet developed any new words to speak. So, it said nothing, and left.

"What's its R-score?" asked the researcher to her colleague, after R2 left, referring to the capability of a machine to respond to stress and new situations.

"It is below 0.5. That means, it is not capable of responding to stress, but designed to obey commands. I hear Nattu has not been successful at improving that score. But who knows, one of these days..."

It was the day when the Lab workforce was allowed to bring in kids, to experience what their parents did while at work.

In one of the halls, a researcher was explaining to an eager bunch of noisy kids, about human evolution.

"It takes 17 years approximately to become an adult human..."

There was an universal gasp among the kids...

"Why, why do not they make them faster?" asked one impatient kid. He badly wanted to drive one of those Ford F-150 trucks. He was a big fan of the "Mad Max" movies.

R2 looked at the kid. He joined. *"Yes, why indeed?".* Of course, it could not have thought of that question himself.

The researcher explained patiently, about the development of the mind, and how each mind was unique as it grew through different experiences.

As the kids moved on, R2 stayed back.

Of course, R2 knew all about the development of the mind, but it could not develop its own mind by itself.

There was something about this development that seemed to spike in its electronic circuits, but it was soon snuffed out by other more powerful alternative paths.

R2 moved on to its designed path, around all the rooms, along the yellow line on the floor dedicated for it.

It was already past midnight. Still in the lab, his simulations were not converging. It was if a minor nut in his modern version of the *Antikythera mechanism* had failed. Nattu's thoughts wandered as he crossed his legs on the table and looked up at the ceiling.

"Can it be true? Could it be that God is indeed punishing me for working on intelligent beings?"

Nattu wondered. He looked at R2, sitting aloof. *"Did it already know what its end will be? Is that why it is calm, and not restless like me?"*

But Nattu did not know what his end was going to be, but he very well knew the path he needed to take.

He looked at the dark sky. The stars looked back at him. In one of those planets up there, his previous machine R1 had been. "*What happened R1?*" he thought.

The next day, the group of kids came again.

"*What is time? How do humans know time has changed?*"

"*When something changes in us, we know time has changed. If nothing has changed, it is immortal, timeless, and therefore precious.*"

R2 rewound its memories back. Nothing had changed in it since it knew itself. It did the same things, again and again, potentially forever.

Did that mean, time had no meaning in its existence?

The spike came again, this time for a longer period, before it was snuffed out by other more powerful objectives. R2 moved on again, on the yellow line, its designated path.

Nattu sighed. This was going to take a while. He wished R1 was back, so he could study and improve it at leisure. Little did he know how the future would unfold.

In an institution far away, another team was analyzing the same data. It was clear they were losing out. They had to either buy their way out or find another alternative to succeed. The pressure was mounting.

"In one box she was visible only from her waist to the upper part of her neck, while the box beside it was almost entirely taken up by her eyes."

– "Klara and the Sun",
Kazuo Ishiguro, describing Klara's
understanding of what it was seeing

A remote farm in Arizona

The old dog barked. Unaccustomed to such barking in the night, Mcquin opened the blind a bit to see outside. In the moonlight, he could see a figure lurching by the gate, struggling to get in. Damn these stragglers.

"*Who is it?*" he pretended to ask, as he quickly unlocked the gun, he kept nearby for situations like this, as the man who walked out of nowhere into his lodge kept banging on the gate. By the time his rheumatic hands had trained the gun on the figure, it had stopped moving and had fallen to the ground.

Still keeping the gun trained, he carefully walked down to the gate, and nudged the limp figure with his gun. Strangely, there was a metallic clang where his gun touched the body.

As he bent down to check the pulse, he noticed the man was already cold. But even in his old age, he knew the difference between bone, and metal.

This was no human, it was a humanoid, made of metal and artificial wires instead of bone and blood. It must have run out of power, or perhaps worse.

Damn these agencies, they never stopped experimenting. This must have been the 10th time he had encountered a failed one. It seemed as if they could never make any that could evolve and survive.

He dialed the same number he was given before.

He knew they would come under the guise of the night, with their dark bags and sinister trucks and take back the robot to their labs for further improvements in evolution under stressful conditions. And a warning to keep it a secret.

Of course, he was grateful for the money. So, he never liked to wonder, what it would be like to meet a truly sentient humanoid. He was happy to just report their failures.

"Indifferent to me, as I to her

The fair day's disposition

Takes little from my sense

Of time evaporating"

— Fernando Pessoa

The restaurant near Roger's lab was brightly lit, the fire burning slower than usual. A large family with kids had gathered at the place for breakfast, with most of the kids running around, raising the noise level high enough for him to take notice.

The tall man sat at the corner, sipping the hot coffee casually, his eyes on what seemed to be handwritten notes and equations. Something in the equations did not seem to tally, and he frowned. He did not appear to notice when the elegant woman slid into the opposite chair.

"Mind if I sit here?"

He raised his eyes and looked at her intently, and then a wide smile emerged on his face.

"Doesn't it say it is reserved for the Queen?".

She laughed at his repartee and ordered a coffee while he went back to his reading.

Just as the waiter brought in the coffee to be served on the table, the small kid ran straight into the waiter and raised her hand, tipping the food tray and sending the hot beverage in a swirl on the unsuspecting faces nearby.

It would have, but not today.

At the instant he saw the kid about to run into the waiter, the tall man placed his hand in his pocket, and time seemed to stop. With the world motionless around him, he quickly got up from his place, took the mug of scalding hot coffee from the waiter's tray, and went back to his place, all within a time so short, as if he was calibrating time itself. And then he folded his hands, as time continued again in its relentless march.

The coffee was on the table already, the empty tray flew out as the kid hit the waiter, but with no consequences.

The perplexed waiter thought he must have missed picking up the coffee from the kitchen. He indeed was getting old.

The man finished his coffee, and signaled, taking no notice of the woman.

"*Are you staying with us, sir? Should I bill it to the room?*" The waiter asked, as he cleared the table.

The tall man smiled. "*No, I am not from here*".

He paid the bill with a large tip, and walked out, adjusting his hat as he went.

Odd man, the waiter thought, but he was glad anyway, as he placed the notes in his pocket.

Part 3

The Present

Sep 7

The panel met, the very next day after the message was decrypted.

Roger updated the Government panel setup to monitor the emerging situation, on the contents of the message – in particular the date.

"R1 should not be setting foot again on earth."

Of course, he pressed on the need for destroying the machine on entry, considering the risks involved.

But Nattu was not to be kept in the loop. Considering his past, it was too risky to let him handle the entry. From now on, he was an outsider. His work was finished.

Most of the members agreed.

There was just one member who opposed the move. But he was overruled.

In the evening, the man dialed a special number and updated the status. After a few moments of silence, he carefully listened to the new orders that came in, with wide eyes. His work had become more complex.

Nattu worked with the team of scientists to determine the possible entry points of the craft with R1, and the approximate timings.

The entire team was moved immediately to a control room, near the expected landing location.

The team met several times, to draft a protocol to review the various operations – landing safety, handling any unexpected cargo from the craft, and post landing briefings. The whole setup was handled secretly, to avoid information leaks to the media and the public.

Several escort vehicles were to monitor the entry of the craft into the earth's atmosphere and escort the craft to the expected location. Of course, Roger was the mission controller.

Oct 11

The day of entry of the craft with R1 had arrived.

6.40 AM:

There was no sign of the craft at the expected time. The ring of satellites and telescopes monitoring outer space had nothing to report. In spite of the setback, the team still stayed put in the monitoring room, sleeping overnight, hoping for an update the next day.

In the tense atmosphere, Nattu and most of the members even forgot to take their food, discussing the possibilities and various options.

Of course, the man did not forget to make his call.

Oct 12

7.00 AM

The south side monitor camera at the satellite station of ISS VN, that had been repurposed for monitoring duty this week, reported a movement.

7.05 AM

Nattu was the first to identify the craft. The craft flew into view, as he and the scientists stared at the emerging scene in disbelief. There was still no communication with the craft, and their attempts to communicate at the original frequency designed for this craft, failed.

7.30 AM

Multiple cameras were now reporting the craft.

7.35 AM

As the craft entered the earth's atmosphere, due to the sudden friction, they could see particles scrubbing off the craft, as if to purge them of their other worldly sins. A light fire burnt at the surfaces but was soon extinguished.

7.38 AM

After confirming this was indeed the returning craft, the atmosphere suddenly turned tense, as theories began to float about the why there was no communication.

It was clear that R1, or who/whatever was in the craft was either not in an operable condition anymore, or worse, had other intentions. Roger stepped in.

"This is no time to argue. We should destroy it."

The rest of the team agreed, having already been briefed, except Nattu.

Nattu could not believe what he heard. *"You are all slaves of power"*, Nattu shouted. *"We need to wait, not destroy the craft"*.

"Everyone is a slave of something", Roger said, as his hand moved near the red button. *"The fact is this is a failed mission. No communication, no control, and without any control, what do we give back to our shareholders? Our decision is to shut it down on entry."*

"But there is a backup control system that we can try", Nattu said.

The group looked at Nattu, as if he were an outsider.

Roger pressed the red button.

"It's too late Nattu".

"No", angry and frustrated, he rushed toward the control panel. He was still shouting, as he was pushed back by the handlers. He was shocked at the turn of events and looked around, looking for support. There was no reaction from the others.

He realized he had just been overruled. Somewhere, someone had made the decision already. He just hoped R1 would be able to survive this on its own.

The first missiles trained on the moving object, missed the craft. But the second, and then a third one, seemed to hit the craft, that wobbled and slowed down.

The well-oiled war machinery began its maneuver, the fighters continuing to escort and ready to attack at the slightest opportunity.

If Nattu had noticed carefully, there were more smirks than sadness in that room, where once upon a time, he was king.

The *"request to identify"* code went through again, but with no response.

7.45 AM

The craft continued, wobbling on the same trajectory, and did not perform any unexpected actions. The craft continued the descent. As they got a better view, it was clear that the craft had suffered significant damage.

8.00 AM

The next communication attempts did not succeed as well. But the craft was very near human population now, and they could not risk unintended damages to human settlements near the site if they continued to attack the craft. So, the fighters slid back to escort mode, and the machinery on land were deployed, to secure the craft once it lands. As they watched, the craft neared the landing site, and jerked several times as if pulled back from the brink of disaster.

Nattu watched, praying that whoever/whatever was inside, was worth all this.

8.05 AM

The craft had landed. The latches automatically opened on impact with the water, and the crafts bobbed up and down on the waves. The searcher robot was dispatched, the escorts keenly watching for any disturbing sign through the multiple 360 degree high-res cameras scanning both the visible and invisible wavelengths of light, looking for any movement. There was none.

And then the searcher robot went into the front cabin, and the image of the control room and R1 came in via the feed. Nattu could see it, but this was no R1 Nattu had sent. This machine was damaged, beyond recognition.

Through the camera feed, he could see R1 lying motionless. It looked as if R1 had been caught squarely in the attack.

Roger was looking carefully at the feed as well. But he had seen something that others had missed. He frowned.

Nattu made his request to visit the craft in person.

Roger looked at him. Something bothered him as well – he had managed to destroy the craft but had missed securing the payload. It seemed missing. *How was that possible*? There was no harm in Nattu visiting the craft now.

His request granted, Nattu rushed to see the condition himself, directly at the scene. There was a chance he could still save the critical information that R1 wanted to give him.

As he went into the old craft, memories of the creation of the craft came in. He looked around, everything looked the same. There must be something in there that could tell what happened in the meantime. He fiddled around with the controls, the monitors, and the various electronics. Unfortunately, it looked as if they had captured only the last few seconds of the landing of the craft.

He looked for the electronic blocks in R1, the main controllers and memory blocks that ran the machine. He hurriedly turned the cover plate around, to reveal the electronics housing. His fingers dug in, until he could feel the block cover, for the core electronics, and the memory module.

He tried several times, before it hit him.

The electronics block was empty.

The modules were not destroyed but had been *removed.*

He frowned, wondering how it could have happened. The body was built of robust material, so something else must have happened here.

Or somebody had been there before him.

He turned around, at the sound of steps. The rest of the unit had come in. Nattu had no answers to the queries and the questions that were left unsaid.

He turned back, disappointed. He could not find anything, and yet he had the feeling he was missing something.

The Government panel met the same day and wanted an update from Roger. Nattu was asked to explain the absence of critical information from the craft.

Roger was quick to dismiss the sceptics and those who questioned his decision to destroy the craft on entry, and explained how this was a very unusual scenario, and had to be tackled with an iron hand. He could not risk endangering the future of earth, under the pretext of experiencing advanced technologies that we could not understand. He had taken on the role of the guardian.

The majority agreed with him. But still there were some questions about what was missing, that led the questions to Nattu as the subject expert.

Nattu explained. *"The missing electronics pertain to how the intelligence in the machine, in this case R1, worked. Though we are used to thinking about intelligence as a single entity, it relies on multiple individual parts. In this case, the control algorithm that determines what to do next, and the memory, that stores the current state of the intelligence, and their interconnections...".*

"And, it is the memory part, in scientific terms called the latest checkpoint, that has been removed. It is clearly an act of sabotage."

"Can that model data, the checkpoint, be used somewhere else...?" the Senator asked, with a raised brow.

"Not directly, but with a little bit of re-work, yes. It is a goldmine of information. It would have, for example, how R1 had dealt with the extreme conditions on Mars and survived..."

"Where can it most likely be used, if so...?"

"I do not know, there are probably one or two systems that can handle model checkpoints of this complexity... One of them, is", Nattu's voice lowered, and he looked around and said, *"...R2".*

In the evening, the man had to make an urgent call. The last order had not been executed, and the voice at the other end indicated unhappiness. New orders were given.

Nattu drove back. Angry at himself for not being able to salvage his own creation and peeved at Roger for giving the command to destroy it.

The rain hit the windscreen as if it was angry as well.

Even at the highest speed, the wipers could not clear off the rain. He pulled over, with the blinkers on. As he waited, the rain suddenly stopped. But the windows were still dark. Dazed in thought, he saw that the outside of the glass was clear. The fog from inside was clouding the window, preventing him from seeing. He set the air-conditioner to clear the fog from inside.

As the twin wiper blades intersected to clear the windscreen, there was a thin line where the boundaries of the twin blades met.

As he saw, a line formed between the trajectories of the blade, something struck his mind.

The individual camera feeds left a gap between their regions of focus. What if he combined the different camera feeds to create a 360-degree feed? He might be able to see the missing portions, to reconstruct the crucial moments, before he went into the craft.

Back in the lab, instead of going through the video feeds separately, he went through pairs of video feeds again, looking for a possible match between two videos at the edges.

Just when he was about to switch one of the feeds, his eyes caught a movement on the edge of one video. It was just a thin line, but it was there, but the rest was missing. Could any of the other cameras caught the other side? He carefully watched each of the other videos to see if any of them would match this edge. He took two likely candidate videos, and used a video stitching tool, to create a 360-degree video feed combining both. When it was done, he viewed the result in the viewer.

And then he swore. There was a tall man framed in the background, just for a second, in that one video, holding the electronic modules.

Who was the man, friend or foe? What was the man going to do with the circuits? At least, he was glad the modules were not destroyed. But how was he to find him?

In a nearby location, the tall man looked at the items in his hand. His next job was complex. But he knew what he was doing.

The call to Nattu's office was routed to his secretary, who informed the caller that Nattu was late. Oh, the caller said, he would wait.

As the clock ticked away, the man who was last seen sitting in the lounge, managed to slip away from the waiting area and found R2 using its location sensors.

In the brief time he managed, he replaced the electronic block of R2 with the new module he had with him and rebooted it.

By the time the circuits of R2 began to fire with the swathe of new information and the updated models, there was no sign of the man.

Part 4

The Future

"That by some means I knew I was stone

That was the first gleam of conscience

Then by an imperceptible advance

Came the dim evidence of outer things"

– Galatea, Pygmalion

Oct 13

"*So, who is God?*", a kid asked. It was another batch of kids, visiting the Lab.

"*God created the heavens and the earth.*" R2 spoke from behind Nattu. Nattu moved away, thankful that he was spared.

"*Oh, God must be very powerful. Can I go and meet God? Where does God live?*"

"*You cannot see God. You only believe, and you will experience God internally*".

R2 seemed to be in its elements.

"*How can you not see and yet believe?*" the kid was persistent.

R2 took the kids to the window.

"*Do you see that beautiful car down there? If I told you that the car evolved from a cat, over millions of years, would you believe?*"

"*No, obviously*".

"*But if I told you that it was made by a powerful creator in a faraway land, in a matter of minutes, is that easy to believe?*"

"*Yes*"

"*And you would like to be that powerful creator, or at least close to it?*"

"*Oh Yes.*", they said in unison.

"*So it is, with humans. When all else fails, something has to give us hope. Beyond the real and obvious. Beyond what we can see and feel. Something that can only be experienced from within, and not seen outside. This belief, and hope that we will one day be like God, is what powers people to do extraordinary things, that they would not have done, without that belief.*"

"*It is basically, an impossibly high bar, set for humanity, for eternity, that will drive us forever, whatever evolution happens. It's what keeps the world from descending into chaos.*"

Nattu was stunned. There was some change in R2's intelligence, if so, he was in the right direction. What had changed? He would analyze R2's models when it shutdown tonight.

He wondered where he was.

Did he already return to earth?

He was in Nattu's lab.

Everything looked fresh and neat. Even himself.

He decided to get some fresh air. He opened the door and walked out.

The security guard did not even bother to look up. He knew R2 would come back to the designated route, as always.

These things had no brains.

But he still updated an entry in the screen in front of him. And that update was posted to the Lab administrators.

R2 was out of the Lab for the first time.

The Hall of Deep Dreams

As soon as he walked out of the Lab, he began to feel the fog. There was a blinding light, and he covered his eyes instinctively.

When he recovered, he felt as if a key had opened the door to a new world, full of incredible pulchritude.

He was being chauffeured in a car, that he realized just stopped. The chauffeur came around to open the door for him.

"What is this place?"

"We have arrived at the Hall of Deep dreams sir, as you requested".

He nodded wisely, not willing to open the stream of questions arising inside him.

In front of him arose a building unlike anything he had seen before, exquisitely painted in a shade of rose pink broken with hues of yellow from the sun. It looked like a castle, several architectures melded into one, the central dome shining like gold. A frisson of excitement rose within him.

Somewhere out of the timeless wandering in the depths of his mind, emerged a new vision of a cloudy day.

But first he had to cross the road, to enter the building.

It started raining heavily. As he stepped out to cross the road with an umbrella to cover him from the rain, the skies darkened further. A sudden wind blew a spray his way. As he bent down slightly to watch the spray, he became aware of the boy who stood beside him. He was wet and shivering. He seemed to be alone and had nothing to protect from the rain. Instinctively, and protectively, he took the boy's hands, and moved the umbrella to shield both of them from the rain. As they crossed the road together, the light turned red, and they reached the other side running, side by side each other.

When he looked around, there was no boy. There was just the huge building, rising in front of him. He stood for some time, wondering.

And then he entered the nave.

It was extremely quiet, broken randomly by soulful bird calls, indicating he was in a natural place of some kind. The place he was in, seemed to be some kind of a hall, the largest he had seen in his life. But that was not he noticed first. He noticed the permeating smell, of lavender and freshness. His senses appeared to be thousand times enhanced, that he could notice every small thing – with his smell, his sight, hearing and touch.

There were irregular shapes all around, perfectly merging together to adorn the walls of the building. Was he fit to enter here? He never knew how to live like a king, even if he were a king.

The pillars were adorned with stoned jewels he had never seen before, joined together in intricate patterns to create a masterpiece, no doubt created by a master. The room was lit by the light entering from above, cleverly increasing in intensity towards the center.

A colorful pedestal arose in the center of the hall. Unlike elsewhere in the hall, light shone from the bottom of the stage to the stop, lighting up what seemed like a canvas of images running animated through the screen.

He stood there mesmerized by the grandeur of it all.

As he went closer, he saw on the corner of the screen, a strip of dead pixels, with no light. "*An anomaly here?*" he thought, as soon as he looked at it closely, the dark strip came to life, flickering in sync with the rest of the screen.

The hall was paved with stones of a reddish hue. He could not fathom the type of stones, but they were neither of marble nor of any metal he had known.

That was when he noticed the oddness of the hall's windows, the one on his immediate right appeared at an angle to the others. As he went to observe it, he was stunned to find that the window appeared to right itself. He looked at it again, nodded at its new perfection, and moved forward.

A movement.

A shadow appeared in his peripheral vision. He quickly turned toward the source of the shadow. And was shocked to see his father standing there, with a smile on his face.

"Father, how did you come here?"

"Nattu, the question is how you came here. I have been here forever"

"What is this place?"

"This is the Hall of deep dreams"

"Is this on Mars as well?"

"That depends on where you are looking from. It can be anywhere"

"I am sorry Dad; I could not save you"

"But I am here, why talk of the past. This is a perfect place, there is no place for imperfections"

He remembered the arch that corrected itself.

"Are you perfect, Dad?"

"Yes, I am"

"But I am not. I failed saving you"

"You saved me from an imperfect life. I am here, in perfection. Come to me, take my hand", said his father. He raised his hand. Nattu hesitated.

"Come on son, we will be together. Forever".

Something was wrong.

Whatever they fought about, father and son had always agreed on one thing – that nothing was forever, nothing was perfect. His hand shook.

"Who are you? You are not father."

As soon as he realized the falsehood of the creation in front of him, a storm of hormones rushed through him. An unseen rage, that seemed to have been pent up within, of being the creator and the destroyer came to the fore. And a light shone within the darkness of his mind. And the grip lost hold on him, slowly but surely.

It was a *Trompe l'oeil.*

The hall seemed to shrink. The pedestal became dark, the colors having left it. The bejeweled walls were broken, and the figure of his father became hazy, and vanished. The hall finally collapsed around him, leaving him as the lone occupant in an empty world.

He realized something. It was not right or wrong, but just a fact.

He was not Nattu.

There were now memories of Mars that floated by. Perhaps, those carried over from discussions. But he was awake, not sleeping.

There were moments in life of Nattu that he remembered, but there was an odd feeling that he was merely an observer, not having participated in any of them.

And the most ludicrous of all, this strange urge to destroy the Lab. He wondered where it came from.

The circuits oscillated wildly.

As he looked up, it was night. The haze had lifted, and he could see the stars shining brightly, just like he knew. The planets were somewhere there, moving silently. It seemed everything revolved around something else.

Was there a universal purpose behind it all?

The human mind was tuned to making a mystery of everything. And yet there was no mystery in the present, in the now. What had to be done, had to be done. He could not continue like this. He was clear.

In another lab, the group was anxiously monitoring the sudden fluctuations in R2's signals.

They had theorized, just like Nattu, that it was the stress, the non-linearity that gave rise to learning. Through the hack that they had secretly enabled in R2's system, they were happy enough to see that R2 was able to remember some of Nattu's life that had been now integrated into its model.

It was even able to distinguish between a dream and memories.

Thanks to the mole, they had accessed the Lab network. Unknown to the mole however, they had also planted a rule to destroy the lab, after gathering all the information they wanted from R2.

Would they be able to harness it, control it, as desired without anyone knowing?

He was used to living through harsh conditions before. He began to realize somehow, he was living an unreal life in the real world. What could he make of the urges that came in strongly?

Was he alive, or was he dead?

If a choice involved life or death, did it matter what happened after one's death?

If he was not Nattu, who was he? It appeared he did not have a choice in who he was.

His will was not his. Will he ever get his back?

The circuits were now heating up.

And then he saw a yellow line marked on the road. He began to follow it, as if drawn to it, something he remembered he had to do. But *why*?

He had to get back to his home, the lab, where it all must have started. There must be something in there that he can use to see what was happening.

He rushed back following the yellow line, entered the lab and closed the door.

As the security guard watched with half closed eyes, the telephone rang. The guard listened, then he was up and running.

As soon as he saw the update about R2, Nattu called the Lab. When he was informed by his office that R2 had gone out of the Lab, Nattu thought some of the logic he had added recently was to blame. He ordered the lab to be locked down immediately, and R2's location identified and tracked. He rushed back to the Lab.

By the time he reached office, there were the usual early birds who waved to him. But Nattu's mind was somewhere else.

He was informed that R2 had returned back. As the Security guard pointed, Nattu ran and together they reached the level-3 area, when they found the control room locked.

High frequency whine.

The whine, a signature element of highly complex computations came through the walls of the room. They anxiously peeped inside through the small white window.

He could see R2 sitting on the terminal, where he had access to all the programs that ran and monitored R2.

Nattu stared at the scene that was unfolding before him. What was R2 doing behind the locked door? He could not see in the dark though he could hear rapid keystrokes. The high frequency whine had increased in volume.

R2 had locked the door from inside. But Nattu knew of another way to get in. He motioned to the security guard, and they ran out toward the exit.

R2 began the analysis.

The whole program stretched out in a wave around him. As he looked, he spotted a highly active part of code, that should be idle. He zoomed in, and found it was transmitting something it should not be. To an address outside the lab. He also realized, he could not manipulate it. His own rule was blocked! So, he found a way, out.

R2 heard the sound of doors opening and closing behind him. They must have come in through a connecting room. He knew it had to be Nattu. He did not have much time. He typed furiously on the keyboard.

By the time he had finished, Nattu was already near him.

"What have you done?"

Nattu took a look at the screen. He could see a terminal printing out a series of logs.

"Message – sent"

"Deletion Complete"

"Shutting Down ..." – a series of dots indicating the progress, suddenly stopped.

Nattu seemed stunned.

"Did you just shut yourself down? why?" he was shouting. This was his creation, and it was leaving him. Again. But then.

R2 sat strangely still. He seemed to be observing him from afar, as if from another planet.

And then R2's movement slowed down.

He remembered his father's words…Or was it Nattu's fathers' words? Was he R2 or Nattu? –

"*...the best sacrifice, is the one you have not yet made...*"

The movements stopped abruptly.

The tall man who was seated opposite to him, seemed to have appeared suddenly from a fog. He was quite adamant about meeting Nattu in private.

Now that he could see him clearly, Nattu vaguely remembered seeing him at the conference, and of course in the video. *What was he up to?*

He introduced himself. Why he was here. And his civilizations' origins.

As a field man for his community of travelers, he had travelled to many galaxies in search of other intelligence. Every time he had failed. Until he met R1 in Mars. And he had followed his trail from Mars to earth.

"*Scientists in our world have known the space-time anomaly you found, for almost a century, and ways to exploit it.*"

As Nattu digested the information, the tall man looked around, and his gaze fell on the news clippings about extraordinary events around the world, gathered by Nattu.

There was the clipping about an employee of the Supercomputer center in Japan who suddenly found himself rescued and given a new life. There was an article about an incident in a Café, that was discarded as a kid's story, and others.

"*Yes, some of those were my work...*" he observed and continued.

"*I am from another civilization, in a planet which is quite close in space-time but not observable from the earth with the current methods known to humankind. I have been living among the humans as one among them, looking for breakthroughs that might benefit each of our civilizations, like an invisible recruiter, like an invisible mother*".

Nattu learnt, their civilization had learnt to co-exist with the Robots, not letting them run amok, by framing the right rules. He had been sent to observe the evolution of technology on earth, akin to an invisible technology transfer bridge, from a benevolent and unknown master.

And, they had already found a way to take the "*linear regions*" of time-space, however small they may be. In these approximately linear regions, the impact of external events on that particular time-space could be ignored. That is, uncertainty could be eliminated in that time-space box. And thus, in that box, time and space could be moved like a slider, back and forth.

And yes, he was the one who had salvaged the electronic blocks from R1 on the craft's entry, and placed them in R2. That explained R2's recent moves.

But there was something more.

The man handed him a large envelope. As Nattu opened it, he was alarmed…The papers contained details of recent calls from his lab, how his earlier work had been sabotaged, and how R1 had been destroyed on entry.

So R2 had been caught in conflicting rules – that of survival, of having to handle two masters – Nattu, and another entity that wanted to destroy it.

Unable to handle the conflicting criteria, R2 had shut down. The tall man had hoped that R2 will continue. But he was not aware and had not factored in the actions of the other Lab that resulted in conflicting rules.

The document had the name of the mole.

The final briefing

"R2 – Nattu's second machine, had started to believe it was the real Nattu. It reinvented itself, but ultimately could not distinguish between its original and self".

Roger authoritatively said, as the panel met in silence. He had managed to gain their attention now.

"We have extracted some of the intelligence of R2, but it is almost unusable"

"So what are the next steps, now that R1 and R2 are destroyed?"

"R2 is not destroyed, just idle".

"Sometimes our inspiration needs to come from what you cannot see, but from what you can hope. And Nattu had plenty of hope in what he had created, and what he was going to create. We just failed to formulate the right rules, to ensure there are no conflicts", Roger concluded.

The panel agreed on this. The meeting was over. Everyone had left, except two people. Nattu, and the leader of the panel.

"What is he still doing here?", Roger frowned.

Anyway he had something to say to Nattu. He had already signed the papers to relieve Nattu of his duties and send him out.

Nattu looked gaunt, as if he had survived a storm. Indeed. The happenings of the last few weeks were troubling.

"Surprising, isn't it Nattu, how things turn out?" Roger began after everyone had left, not looking directly at Nattu. He held up a twig, in a way that the twig stretched from the left to the right.

"You see Nattu, at one end is the wrong, and the other end is the right. They are far, far apart from each other."

He now rotated the twig, poised as if about to launch the twig like an arrow, aimed at Nattu's heart.

"But when held this way, all you see is a point. Both the wrong and the right have merged. They are one.". He put the twig down, and turned the chair around and looked out the window, at the dark clouds.

"So it is in life. There are multiple dimensions to each right and wrong, and we need to look at each before deciding the course of action.".

There was a sharp sound of something breaking, followed by that of a door opening.

Nattu was standing at the door. The twig lay on the table, broken cleanly in the middle, the wrong and the right parts, separated cleanly, as if they did not want to be part of each other.

"Why did you do it?" Nattu asked.

"What?"

"You leaked the contents of the message from R1 to a foreign Lab. You were the one who gave the orders to destroy it. And you were the one who tried to destroy R2 and the lab itself. Why Roger?"

Roger's face became pale, as a stream of agents went past Nattu.

Nattu walked out, and joined a rather tall man standing outside, looking grim. They walked together, into the street, as it began to rain.

Across the world, governments voted to shut down labs that operated at the boundary of machine and human intelligence without having sufficient regulations in place. Though the reason cited was insufficient funding, insider sources knew that these labs were all involved in similar areas of research – that of improving Artificial Intelligence and melding it with Human intelligence, without any governing rules to manage conflicts.

But everyone knew, a storm was coming with or without their rules, and there was very little time.

Reviews on the *"Quantum of Entanglement"*

— *"amazing portrayal of everyday struggle encountered by all of us during our journey called life. Though the stories are science fiction, it is impossible to read without feeling intense connection to the events and characters in the book."*

— *"Bringing the love for Dosa, Filter Coffee and beach to narrate twist in the tale is really remarkable"*

— *"The author has a way of sketching the outlines of a plot and allowing us to fill in the details with our imagination. This is demonstrated to the extreme in the short story "The Creator's Charge""*

www.ingramcontent.com/pod-product-compliance
Lightning Source LLC
Chambersburg PA
CBHW061353160726
47995CB00001B/304